MY FIRST LITTLE HOUSE BOOKS

COUNTY FAIR

ADAPTED FROM THE LITTLE HOUSE BOOKS

By Laura Ingalls Wilder

Illustrated by Jody Wheeler

HARPERCOLLINS PUBLISHERS

For Armani
—J.W.

Special thanks to Larry House and the Almanzo and Laura Ingalls Wilder Home Association. Thanks also to Roy Hall of the Franklin County Agricultural Society for his research on county fairs. Art direction by Renée Graef.

The illustrations in this book were prepared with the help of Doris Ettlinger.

Illustrations for the My First Little House Books are
inspired by the work of Garth Williams with his
permission, which we gratefully acknowledge.

Once upon a time, a little boy named Almanzo lived in a farmhouse in the New York State countryside. He lived with his Father, his Mother, his big brother, Royal, and his two big sisters, Eliza Jane and Alice.

Early one morning they all set out for the County Fair. Father placed under the buggy seat the box of pickles and preserves and jellies that Eliza Jane and Alice had made. Alice was taking her woolwork embroidery, too. But Almanzo's pumpkin had gone to the Fair the day before in the wagon. It was too big to fit in the buggy.

The roads were filled with people in their best clothes all going to the Fair. Mother and Royal and the girls got out of the buggy at the Fair Grounds, but Almanzo rode on with Father to the sheds and helped unhitch the horses.

Almanzo wanted to see the animals first. He and Father went past the tall grand-stand and the church building where Mother and the girls were helping to prepare dinner. Everywhere men were shouting: "Step this way, only ten cents!" and "Prizes for all!"

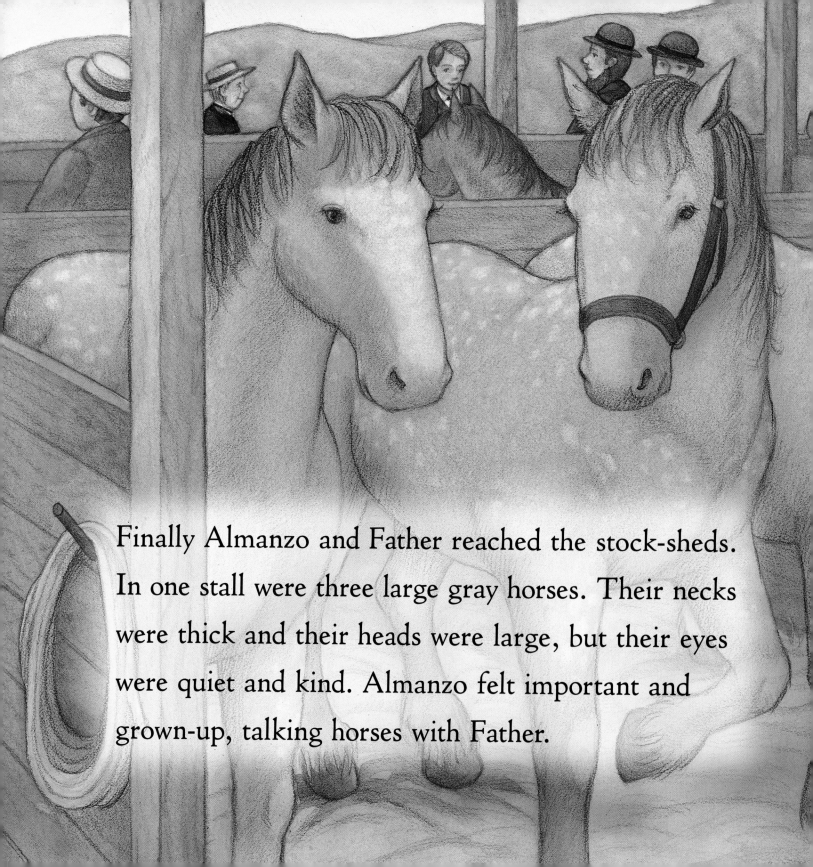

Finally Almanzo and Father reached the stock-sheds.
In one stall were three large gray horses. Their necks
were thick and their heads were large, but their eyes
were quiet and kind. Almanzo felt important and
grown-up, talking horses with Father.

Next to the horses there was a crowd of men and boys around a stall. Not even Father could see what was in it. Almanzo squeezed between the legs until he came to the bars of the stall. Inside it were two black creatures he had never seen before. They were something like horses, but they were not horses. Their ears were like rabbits' ears, and their tails were almost bare.

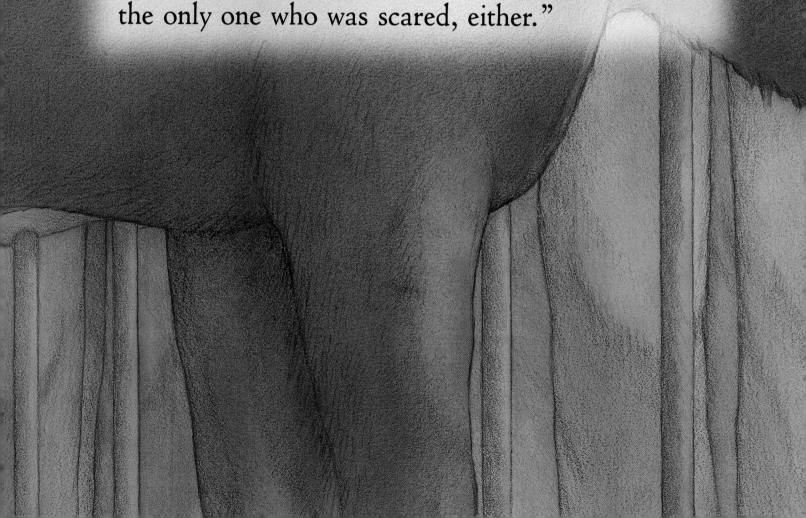

While Almanzo stared, one of those creatures pointed its ears at him and stretched out its neck and roared: "Eeeeeeeeee, aw! Heeeeeee, haw!"

Almanzo yelled and hurried back to Father. "It's only a mule, son," Father said. "And you're not the only one who was scared, either."

Almanzo and Father looked at the cattle and the young steers and the sturdy oxen. They looked at the big white hogs and the smaller black hogs. Then they looked at sheep. Almanzo had not seen his pumpkin yet. But it was time to eat, and Almanzo was hungry.

The church dining-room was already crowded. Everyone was talking and laughing, but Almanzo just ate. He ate ham and chicken and turkey. He ate potatoes and gravy, succotash, baked beans and onions and bread. He ate pumpkin pie and custard pie and vinegar pie. There were berry pies and cream pies and raisin pies, but he could not eat one bite more.

At last it was time for the pumpkins to be judged. Almanzo saw at once that his pumpkin was the largest of them all. He tried not to care too much about the prize. But he wished everyone knew that the biggest pumpkin was his.

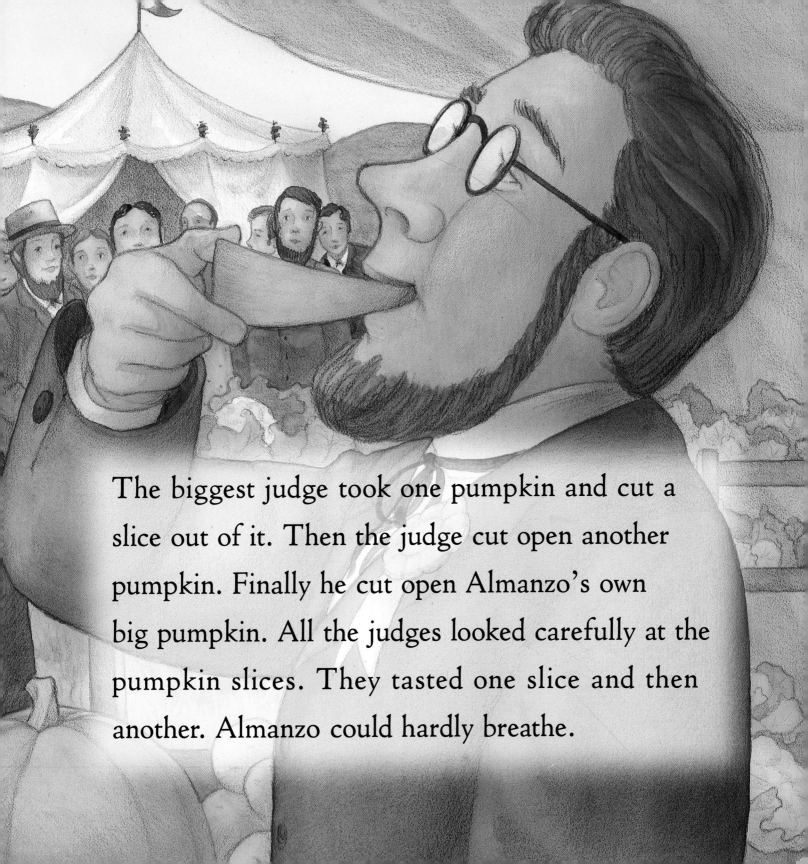

The biggest judge took one pumpkin and cut a slice out of it. Then the judge cut open another pumpkin. Finally he cut open Almanzo's own big pumpkin. All the judges looked carefully at the pumpkin slices. They tasted one slice and then another. Almanzo could hardly breathe.

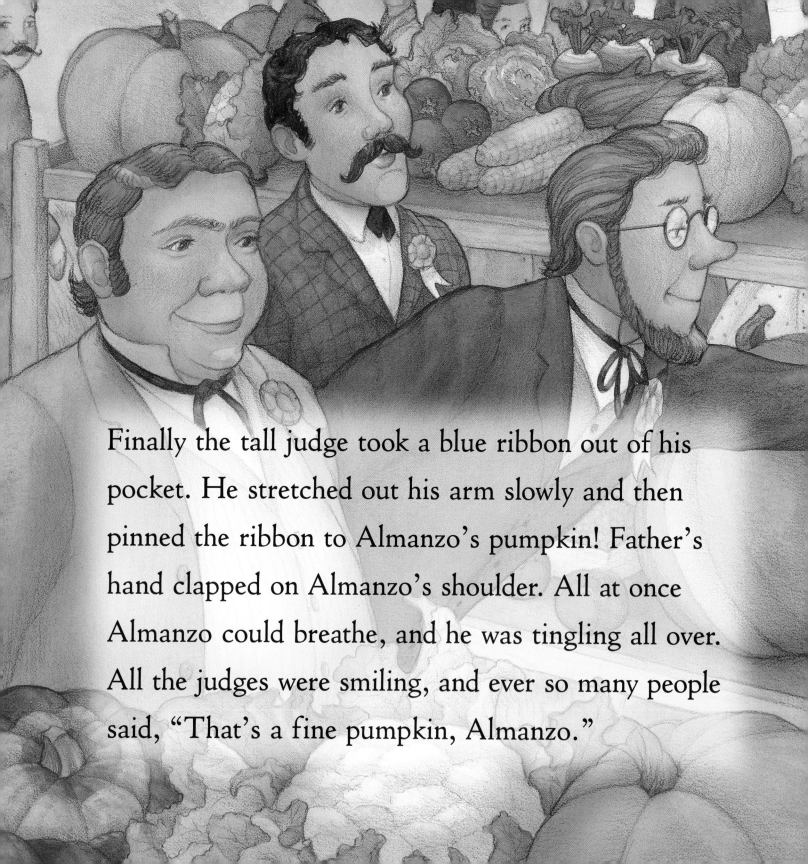

Finally the tall judge took a blue ribbon out of his pocket. He stretched out his arm slowly and then pinned the ribbon to Almanzo's pumpkin! Father's hand clapped on Almanzo's shoulder. All at once Almanzo could breathe, and he was tingling all over. All the judges were smiling, and ever so many people said, "That's a fine pumpkin, Almanzo."

Afterward Almanzo went walking with Father through the fair. They watched the foot-races, and the jumping contests, and the throwing contests.

The boys from town were in all the contests, but the farmer boys won, almost every time. Almanzo kept remembering his prize pumpkin and feeling good.

Driving home that night, they all felt good. Alice's woolwork had won first prize, and Eliza Jane had a red ribbon for her pickles and preserves, and Alice had a blue ribbon for her jellies. Father said the Wilder family had done itself proud that day.

Almanzo was the proudest of all.